COMING HOME
A DOG'S TRUE STORY

Illustrated by Lisa Kopper
Story by Ted Harriott

Lynx · London · 1988

Text copyright © Ted Harriott 1985
Illustrations copyright © LisaKopper 1985

First published in Great Britain in 1985
by Victor Gollancz Ltd
This Lynx edition published in 1988
by Victor Gollancz Ltd

British Library Cataloguing in Publication Data
Kopper, Lisa
 Coming home.
 I. Title II. Harriott, Ted, *1933-*
823′.914[J]

ISBN 0-575-04333-4

Printed and bound in Hong Kong by Imago Publishing Ltd

My first master was an old man called Paddy. He had a smoky smell about him as if he had sat hunched over a fire for years.

The floor-boards in our room were hard and splintery but I was not allowed on the chairs or the bed. He was strict about the rules, but he was kind to me. He fed me most days and only shouted when I got something wrong.

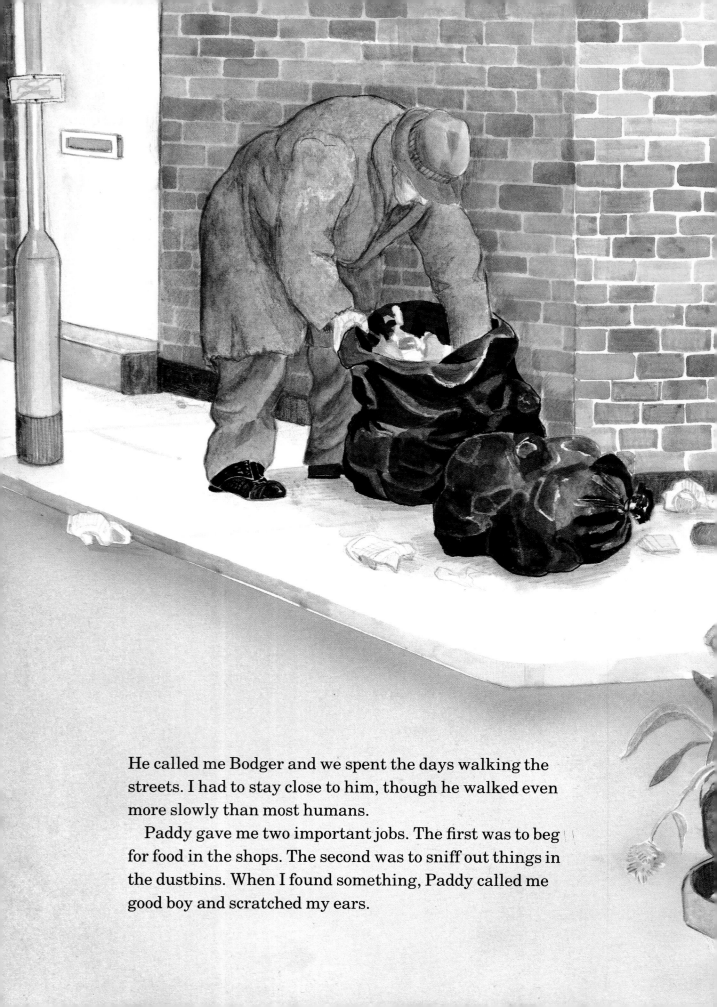

He called me Bodger and we spent the days walking the
streets. I had to stay close to him, though he walked even
more slowly than most humans.

Paddy gave me two important jobs. The first was to beg
for food in the shops. The second was to sniff out things in
the dustbins. When I found something, Paddy called me
good boy and scratched my ears.

Sometimes, after we had eaten, Paddy would say in his happy voice, "Come on then, my old Bodger. Let's go up the pub and have a drink." There were always other people at the pub, drinking from pint mugs and laughing loudly. Paddy told them stories about the old days and they said, "Have another one, Paddy." I did tricks for them and they gave me pieces of pie and sausage.

Paddy and I would go home very late on those special nights.

But, one winter, Paddy suddenly became tired and didn't want to go for walks with me any more.

I saw that he was frightened when a young woman came to our room and told him, "You will have to go into hospital for a long time. We'll have your old dog taken care of."

"Taken care of!" shouted Paddy. "Put down, you mean."

Paddy was trembling when the woman left. He pulled me on to his bed and held me in his arms – something he had never done before. I was worried. I wasn't allowed on the bed.

Then he got up, closed the door and started piling things against it. I whined because he was so upset. I tried to tell him that soon it would be spring again, but he wouldn't listen. He just lay down and went to sleep.

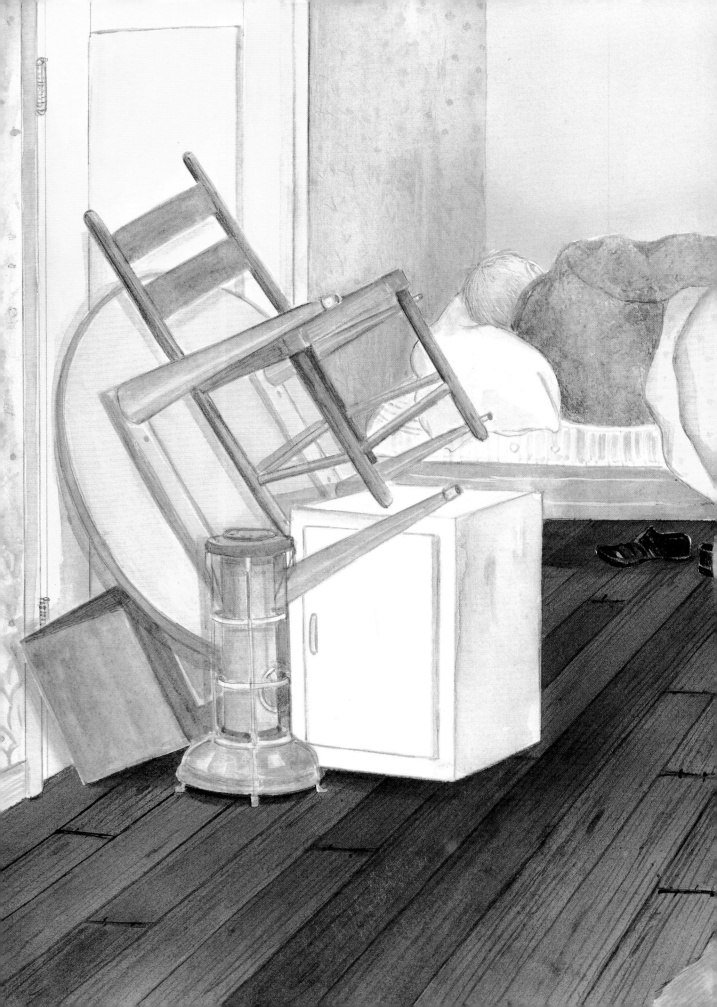

Next morning when I woke up I tried to get Paddy out of bed to open the door for me. He just patted my head. I was hungry and thirsty, but I soon found out how to lap a little water from the dripping tap over the sink.

I was pleased with my discovery and ran to tell Paddy so that he could get some. I nosed his ear. It was cold and he did not move. He had gone away somewhere and I knew he would never come back.

I howled and howled, but no one came for days. At last, policemen smashed down the door. I was so weak that I could only just get up to wag my tail and greet them.

They took me to a place called the Dogs' Home and locked me in a cage with a stone floor. There were rows of cages full of dogs. It was such a sad place. We all knew that if we were not rescued soon we would be taken through the door at the end of the corridor. Dogs never came back from there.

I would surely go through that door. Who would want me now? I was all skin and bones, and had lost a lot of hair.

After a few days I watched a woman walk along the corridor. The other dogs all called out to her, "Take me! Take me!" But she came straight to my cage. And then I recognised her. She was one of the people Paddy and I used to see on our walks. The attendant opened the cage door – I was saved!

For the next few hours I wasn't sure that I liked being saved. The woman took me first to a man she called the vet, who stuck a needle into me, bathed and powdered me.

They were getting me ready for someone to see me.

I began to understand what it was all about when she told the vet, "I don't know what I'll do if he says I can't keep the dog."

Then she took me to her home, where we sat and waited. At last a man arrived. He stared hard at me and I held my breath. He *had* to let me stay. I lay under the table peeping out. I couldn't take my eyes off him as the woman told him about me. I hoped he understood how frightened I was that I might be sent back to the Dogs' Home.

"Can we keep him?" asked the woman.

It seemed a long time before he answered, "All right. We'll see how it goes."

I wriggled out of my hiding place and he held his hand out to me. I sniffed it and then licked it gently. He was my new master. But I wondered if he could ever love me as much as Paddy had.

Then I had an idea. I asked if I could go out and my mistress opened the door for me. I hunted about and my nose led me to a metal dustbin. The smell was strong and exciting. I reached in and took something out.

I hurried upstairs again and scratched at the door. When my master opened it, I wagged my tail and dropped my gift at his feet.

"He's brought us a present," said my new mistress as she hugged me.

"A smelly old lump of cheese," said my master. He was smiling and he patted me, running his hands along my sides. "He's very thin and his skin's in a bad state," he said. "He's been through rough times but he'll be all right now."

He thought for a minute . . .

"Let's call him Job."

For Job's other helpers, Nancy, Marcia and Poppy

Job, (which rhymes with "robe"), was named after the Biblical character whose patience helped him to endure many trials. He was rescued from a dogs' home in 1979 by a neighbour and two of her friends who had heard about the death of Job's old master. One of these friends was the artist Lisa Kopper, who illustrated *Coming Home*. Ted Harriott, the author of the story, pieced together the facts with the help of other people who lived in the area.

When he was rescued, Job was in a sorry state. He had lost most of his hair and he could not digest normal dog food. He had spent at least a week locked in a room with his dead master when the police arrived. However, a series of injections and a diet of chicken and rice with vitamins cured most of his problems.

Job is now a happy, healthy dog who requires several long walks each day, and who still enjoys an occasional meal of chicken and rice.